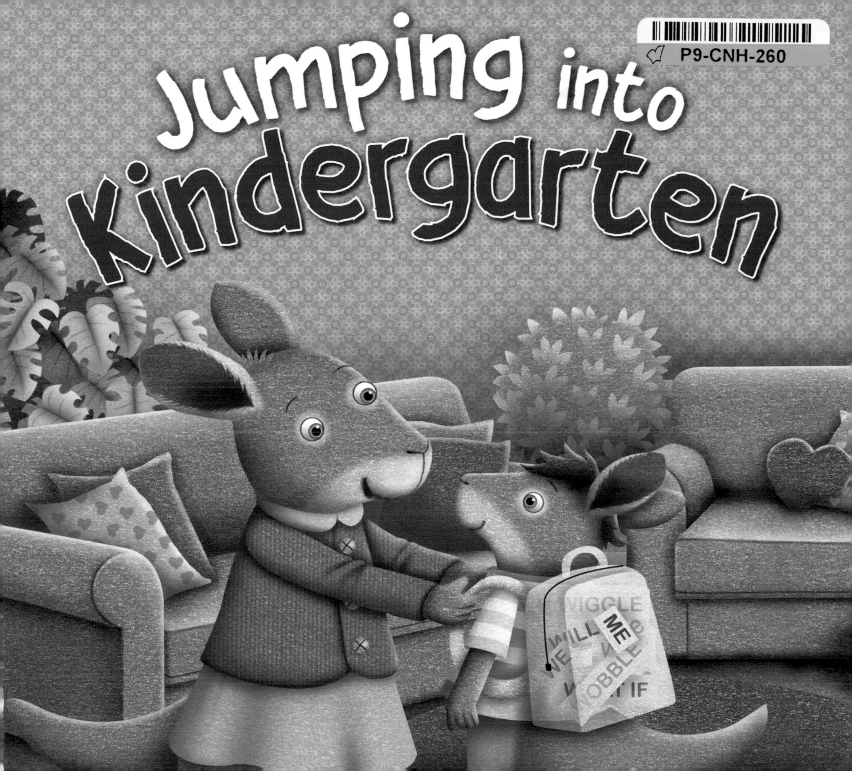

Jumping into Kindergarten

For all the little Roos out there
who are ready to jump!

DUPLICATION AND COPYRIGHT

NATIONAL CENTER for
YOUTH ISSUES

P.O. Box 22185 • Chattanooga, TN 37422-2185
423.899.5714 • 866.318.6294
fax: 423.899.4547 • www.ncyi.org

ISBN: 978-1-937870-43-0
Library of Congress Control Number: 2017945751
© 2017 National Center for Youth Issues, Chattanooga, TN
All rights reserved.
Written by: Julia Cook and Laura A. Jana, M.D.
Illustrations by: James Newman Gray
Design by: Phillip W. Rodgers
Contributing Editors: Jennifer Deshler and Beth Spencer Rabon
Published by National Center for Youth Issues • Softcover
Printed at Starkey Printing, Chattanooga, Tennessee, U.S.A., September 2018

I'm jumping into kindergarten.
Ready...Get set...GO!
I can't wait to meet my teachers,
and show them what I know.

But I'm kinda scared to go there.
I'm not sure what we will do.
Is it going to be like preschool?
Will the carpet still be blue?

What if I don't like it?
What if I don't know what to wear?
What if I can't answer my
teacher's questions?
What if the other kids don't share?

And what if they laugh at my HAIR?

What if? What if?
What if?

Don't worry, you'll be Ok!

You already have all the skills you need to figure out your way.

I do know how to button and zip,
and I know what it means to rhyme.

I'm getting really good at bouncing a ball,
because I do it all the time.

Yes! And you're learning to count, cut, and trace, and practicing your letters and colors.

But what's really going to make you a star, are skills that are different from the others!

You know, the skills in your **invisible backpack**.

Oh yeah! Those are my

SUPER COOL SKILLS,

that are sometimes hard to see.

But when I remember to use them,
they make me a better me!

I have **ME** skills and **WE** skills,
WHY skills and **WILL** skills,
and skills you like to call **WIGGLE**.

My **WOBBLE** and **WHAT IF** skills
help me do lots of things.

Some of them make us giggle.

My **ME** skills help me pay attention,
and control how I act, think, and feel.

They help me keep track of what I should be doing.
ME skills are a really BIG deal!

Whenever I use my **WE** skills,
it's easier for me to share.

They help me play well with others,
and show them how much I care.

And I don't ever make fun of other people's HAIR!

I wonder about a lot of stuff, so I always ask, *when, where, why, what,* and *how?*

My **WHY** skills help me make sense of the world.

"Hey mom…is a bull still a cow?"

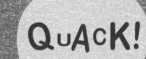

QuAcK!

Why does that switch
make the lights turn on?

What kind of shoes are those?

Where are we going?
When will we get there?

What's that thing in your nose?

Some days when I don't feel so brave,
I really start to wonder.

Why do I have to go to kindergarten anyway?
So, I find a bed to hide under.

You don't **have** to go to kindergarten...
You **get** to go to kindergarten!

Oh. I like "get to's" a whole lot better!

17

My **WILL** skills tell me to always keep trying.

When things get hard, I don't quit.

I try and try, and then I try harder.

I don't like quitting one bit!

Instead of saying,

"I just can't do it!!"

I say,

"I just can't do it **yet!**"

I **LOVE** to move around and explore,
so my favorite skill is **WIGGLE**.

I can jump into things, reach for the stars,
and bend and stretch and jiggle!

Jiggle!   **Jiggle!**

Jiggle!

I like to reach out and touch things,
just to see how they feel.

My **WIGGLE** skills make my brain work better,
and my world becomes much more real.

Wiggle!

Wiggle!

Wiggle!

Sometimes I **WIGGLE** and jiggle so much,
that I **WOBBLE** and then I fall down.

But I dust myself off and get right back up,
and smile instead of frown!

My **WOBBLE** skills help me take chances.
I know what to do when things go wrong.

I'm learning by making lots of great mistakes,
'cause my **WOBBLE** skills help me grow strong.

My **WHAT IF** skills make playtime extra fun!
My imagination is fantastic!
I wonder what I could do if I had superpowers?
What if skyscrapers were made out of plastic?

What if mountains were made out of chocolate?

What if I lived on the moon?

What if I could teach pigs how to fly?

What if a robot could clean my room?

See! Look at all the stuff you already know,
and all the things your skills help you do.

I bet your teachers just can't wait
to get to know the **amazing** you!

Now pack up that invisible backpack of yours.

Take it with you wherever you go.

Strap it on tight. It's time to jump!

Get ready...Get set...**GROW!**

Why are you wearing that hat to school?

Because I don't want anyone to make fun of my **HAIR!**

Get Ready,
Get Set...GROW!

It's Time to JUMP!

Tips for Parents and Educators

Starting kindergarten is a major event in every child's life. As parents, educators and CEO's (Chief *Engagement* Officers), we have the opportunity to equip our children with a set of twenty-first century skills – called "QI" (pronounced *key*) Skills – that can help them better prepare for what lies ahead. Here are a few tips to help your child successfully *and* happily "JUMP" into kindergarten.

ME SKILLS: Focusing attention on self-awareness and self-control

Learning self-awareness and self-control takes time. Be consistent in establishing predictable routines. Talk, sing, and read to your child about emotions – all of which will help to build your child's emotional vocabulary and encourage emotional awareness and expression. Remember that developing self-awareness and self-control takes practice, and is much easier to master when children are well rested and get to see their parents and other adults model these behaviors.

WE SKILLS: The "people skills" needed to communicate, collaborate, and play well with others

WE Skills involve learning to read other people and understand how they think and feel. Model and practice active listening, demonstrate what it means to play nice, and encourage dress-up play to foster imagination and help children learn to "walk in someone else's shoes." By making it a daily routine to think about and help others in various ways, your child is also taking foundational steps towards developing empathy and WE Skills.

WHY SKILLS: Curiosity and seeing the world as a question mark

Young children are naturally curious and ask many questions. You can help your child better understand how the world works by encouraging their questions and answering with truthful, age-appropriate information and explanations. When you don't know the answer, don't hesitate to say, "I don't know," – and then commit to helping find it. As children get older, start asking them more thought-provoking questions that relate to their world. By gradually increasing your Q/A ratio (questions asked to answers given) your child will become increasingly skilled at searching out and finding answers independently.

WILL SKILLS: Self-motivation and drive

As tempting as it may be to reward young children for every job well done, remember that your ultimate goal is to raise a child who is self motivated and learns to work hard for the sake of achieving goals, rather than gifts. You can promote WILL Skills by focusing your attention on effort, rather than just achievement; and on praising perseverance rather than performance. It certainly helps to model a stick-with-it attitude yourself, and give your child plenty of time to practice. Help your child learn that achieving success is always a work in progress, and that "becoming is better than being!"

WIGGLE SKILLS: Physical and intellectual restlessness

Children learn by doing, so be sure to recognize WIGGLE when you see it! Children need to run around in, touch, and get a hands-on feel for the world. Rather than emphasizing the look-but-don't-touch approach, give your child plenty of wiggle room and the opportunity to appropriately run free and explore, both indoors and outdoors. For children who really like to wiggle a lot, remember that even reading aloud can be adapted to be a more active activity. After all, your ultimate goal isn't just to work the wiggles out, but rather to help your child learn to put their wiggles to work!

WOBBLE SKILLS: Agility, adaptability, and making great mistakes

Becoming skilled at WOBBLing means helping your child learn to make great mistakes. Instead of focusing on getting things right the first time, and being the fastest or the best, children need time and encouragement to learn how to get things wrong, think things through, practice, and figure things out for themselves. It can be difficult to watch your child get frustrated and fail, but focus your attention on wobble-proofing (i.e. safety-proofing) your child's environment and offering words of encouragement. Bottom line: don't forget to celebrate the great mistakes and failures that will eventually lead to your child's success.

WHAT IF SKILLS: Fostering creativity and imagining a world of possibilities

Young children are naturally creative and imaginative, which makes the WHAT IF Skills especially fun and easy to foster. Playing with "open-ended" toys – ones that don't come with step-by-step instructions - are especially good for inspiring children to come up with creative ways of using them. Telling fanciful stories and reading books to your children early and often allows their imaginations to run free. Making sure your child also spends time unplugged from electronics helps provide valuable WHAT IF-enhancing time to be bored, since boredom is a great way to encourage creative thinking and WHAT IF Skill development. Finally, keep in mind that while it is certainly important to learn how to follow rules, it's also important not to have so many rules that they stifle your child's desire or ability to learn how to think outside the box and color outside the lines.